THE BOXCAR CHILDREN® MYSTERIES

THE BOXCAR CHILDREN
SURPRISE ISLAND
THE YELLOW HOUSE MYSTERY
MYSTERY RANCH
MIKE'S MYSTERY
BLUE BAY MYSTERY
THE WOODSHED MYSTERY
THE LIGHTHOUSE MYSTERY
MOUNTAIN TOP MYSTERY
SCHOOLHOUSE MYSTERY
CABOOSE MYSTERY
HOUSEBOAT MYSTERY
SNOWBOUND MYSTERY
TREE HOUSE MYSTERY
BICYCLE MYSTERY
MYSTERY IN THE SAND
MYSTERY BEHIND THE WALL
BUS STATION MYSTERY
BENNY UNCOVERS A MYSTERY
THE HAUNTED CABIN MYSTERY
THE DESERTED LIBRARY MYSTERY
THE ANIMAL SHELTER MYSTERY
THE OLD MOTEL MYSTERY
THE MYSTERY OF THE HIDDEN PAINTING
THE AMUSEMENT PARK MYSTERY
THE MYSTERY OF THE MIXED-UP ZOO
THE CAMP-OUT MYSTERY
THE MYSTERY GIRL
THE MYSTERY CRUISE
THE DISAPPEARING FRIEND MYSTERY
THE MYSTERY OF THE SINGING GHOST
THE MYSTERY IN THE SNOW
THE PIZZA MYSTERY
THE MYSTERY HORSE
THE MYSTERY AT THE DOG SHOW
THE CASTLE MYSTERY
THE MYSTERY OF THE LOST VILLAGE
THE MYSTERY ON THE ICE
THE MYSTERY OF THE PURPLE POOL
THE GHOST SHIP MYSTERY
THE MYSTERY IN WASHINGTON, DC
THE CANOE TRIP MYSTERY
THE MYSTERY OF THE HIDDEN BEACH
THE MYSTERY OF THE MISSING CAT
THE MYSTERY AT SNOWFLAKE INN

THE MYSTERY ON STAGE
THE DINOSAUR MYSTERY
THE MYSTERY OF THE STOLEN MUSIC
THE MYSTERY AT THE BALL PARK
THE CHOCOLATE SUNDAE MYSTERY
THE MYSTERY OF THE HOT AIR BALLOON
THE MYSTERY BOOKSTORE
THE PILGRIM VILLAGE MYSTERY
THE MYSTERY OF THE STOLEN BOXCAR
THE MYSTERY IN THE CAVE
THE MYSTERY ON THE TRAIN
THE MYSTERY AT THE FAIR
THE MYSTERY OF THE LOST MINE
THE GUIDE DOG MYSTERY
THE HURRICANE MYSTERY
THE PET SHOP MYSTERY
THE MYSTERY OF THE SECRET MESSAGE
THE FIREHOUSE MYSTERY
THE MYSTERY IN SAN FRANCISCO
THE NIAGARA FALLS MYSTERY
THE MYSTERY AT THE ALAMO
THE OUTER SPACE MYSTERY
THE SOCCER MYSTERY
THE MYSTERY IN THE OLD ATTIC
THE GROWLING BEAR MYSTERY
THE MYSTERY OF THE LAKE MONSTER
THE MYSTERY AT PEACOCK HALL
THE WINDY CITY MYSTERY
THE BLACK PEARL MYSTERY
THE CEREAL BOX MYSTERY
THE PANTHER MYSTERY
THE MYSTERY OF THE QUEEN'S JEWELS
THE STOLEN SWORD MYSTERY
THE BASKETBALL MYSTERY
THE MOVIE STAR MYSTERY
THE MYSTERY OF THE PIRATE'S MAP
THE GHOST TOWN MYSTERY
THE MYSTERY OF THE BLACK RAVEN
THE MYSTERY IN THE MALL
THE MYSTERY IN NEW YORK
THE GYMNASTICS MYSTERY
THE POISON FROG MYSTERY
THE MYSTERY OF THE EMPTY SAFE
THE HOME RUN MYSTERY
THE GREAT BICYCLE RACE MYSTERY

THE MYSTERY OF THE WILD PONIES
THE MYSTERY IN THE COMPUTER GAME
THE HONEYBEE MYSTERY
THE MYSTERY AT THE CROOKED HOUSE
THE HOCKEY MYSTERY
THE MYSTERY OF THE MIDNIGHT DOG
THE MYSTERY OF THE SCREECH OWL
THE SUMMER CAMP MYSTERY
THE COPYCAT MYSTERY
THE HAUNTED CLOCK TOWER MYSTERY
THE MYSTERY OF THE TIGER'S EYE
THE DISAPPEARING STAIRCASE MYSTERY
THE MYSTERY ON BLIZZARD MOUNTAIN
THE MYSTERY OF THE SPIDER'S CLUE
THE CANDY FACTORY MYSTERY
THE MYSTERY OF THE MUMMY'S CURSE
THE MYSTERY OF THE STAR RUBY
THE STUFFED BEAR MYSTERY
THE MYSTERY OF ALLIGATOR SWAMP
THE MYSTERY AT SKELETON POINT
THE TATTLETALE MYSTERY
THE COMIC BOOK MYSTERY
THE GREAT SHARK MYSTERY
THE ICE CREAM MYSTERY
THE MIDNIGHT MYSTERY
THE MYSTERY IN THE FORTUNE COOKIE
THE BLACK WIDOW SPIDER MYSTERY
THE RADIO MYSTERY
THE MYSTERY OF THE RUNAWAY GHOST
THE FINDERS KEEPERS MYSTERY
THE MYSTERY OF THE HAUNTED BOXCAR
THE CLUE IN THE CORN MAZE
THE GHOST OF THE CHATTERING BONES
THE SWORD OF THE SILVER KNIGHT
THE GAME STORE MYSTERY
THE MYSTERY OF THE ORPHAN TRAIN
THE VANISHING PASSENGER
THE GIANT YO-YO MYSTERY
THE CREATURE IN OGOPOGO LAKE
THE ROCK 'N' ROLL MYSTERY
THE SECRET OF THE MASK
THE SEATTLE PUZZLE
THE GHOST IN THE FIRST ROW
THE BOX THAT WATCH FOUND
A HORSE NAMED DRAGON
THE GREAT DETECTIVE RACE
THE GHOST AT THE DRIVE-IN MOVIE

THE MYSTERY OF THE TRAVELING TOMATOES
THE SPY GAME
THE DOG-GONE MYSTERY
THE VAMPIRE MYSTERY
SUPERSTAR WATCH
THE SPY IN THE BLEACHERS
THE AMAZING MYSTERY SHOW
THE PUMPKIN HEAD MYSTERY
THE CUPCAKE CAPER
THE CLUE IN THE RECYCLING BIN
MONKEY TROUBLE
THE ZOMBIE PROJECT
THE GREAT TURKEY HEIST
THE GARDEN THIEF
THE BOARDWALK MYSTERY
THE MYSTERY OF THE FALLEN TREASURE
THE RETURN OF THE GRAVEYARD GHOST
THE MYSTERY OF THE STOLEN SNOWBOARD
THE MYSTERY OF THE WILD WEST BANDIT
THE MYSTERY OF THE SOCCER SNITCH
THE MYSTERY OF THE GRINNING GARGOYLE
THE MYSTERY OF THE MISSING POP IDOL
THE MYSTERY OF THE STOLEN DINOSAUR BONES
THE MYSTERY AT THE CALGARY STAMPEDE
THE SLEEPY HOLLOW MYSTERY
THE LEGEND OF THE IRISH CASTLE
THE CELEBRITY CAT CAPER
HIDDEN IN THE HAUNTED SCHOOL
THE ELECTION DAY DILEMMA
THE DOUGHNUT WHODUNIT
THE ROBOT RANSOM
THE LEGEND OF THE HOWLING WEREWOLF
THE DAY OF THE DEAD MYSTERY
THE HUNDRED-YEAR MYSTERY
THE SEA TURTLE MYSTERY
SECRET ON THE THIRTEENTH FLOOR
THE POWER DOWN MYSTERY
MYSTERY AT CAMP SURVIVAL
THE MYSTERY OF THE FORGOTTEN FAMILY
THE SKELETON KEY MYSTERY
SCIENCE FAIR SABOTAGE
NEW! THE GREAT GREENFIELD BAKE-OFF
NEW! THE BEEKEEPER MYSTERY

THE BOXCAR CHILDREN®

CREATED BY
GERTRUDE CHANDLER WARNER

BOOK

159

THE BEEKEEPER MYSTERY

ILLUSTRATED BY
ANTHONY VanARSDALE

ALBERT WHITMAN & COMPANY
CHICAGO, ILLINOIS

ISBN 978-0-8075-0823-7 (hardcover)
ISBN 978-0-8075-0824-4 (paperback)
ISBN 978-0-8075-0826-8 (ebook)

Printed in the United States of America
10 9 8 7 6 5 4 3 2 1 LB 26 25 24 23 22 21

Illustrations by Anthony VanArsdale

Visit The Boxcar Children® online at www.boxcarchildren.com.
For more information about Albert Whitman & Company,
visit our website at www.albertwhitman.com.

Contents

1. The Honeybee Emergency   1

2. Missing!   12

3. Secrets in the Storeroom   26

4. Combing Honey, Brushing Bees   36

5. Stolen!   47

6. Four Eggs-pert Detectives   57

7. The Spinning Spaceship   66

8. Flashlight in the Dark   77

9. Connecting the Clues   86

10. Noah's Surprise   97

The Honeybee Emergency

Benny Alden lay on his back, staring at the living room ceiling. Watch, the family's wirehaired terrier, was curled next to him. It was the last week of summer vacation. Benny was wondering what he and his siblings would do this week when the phone rang.

"Can somebody please get that?" called Grandfather.

Benny scrambled up and answered the phone. "Hello?" he said.

"Benny?" asked a woman. Benny thought the voice sounded familiar. "It's Laura," she said. "Laura Shea. I know we've talked about a visit to the farm, and I wondered if you and your siblings could come this week. Are you busy?"

"No," said Benny. "We're just waiting for school to start."

"Perfect," said Laura. "I could really use your help with an emergency. A honeybee emergency!"

***

"I've never heard of a honeybee emergency," said Jessie Alden. The twelve-year-old girl rode in the back seat of the car with her six-year-old brother, Benny, and ten-year-old sister, Violet. They were on their way to Laura's farm. Her big brother, Henry, sat up front with Grandfather. "What exactly *is* a honeybee emergency?" Jessie asked.

"I don't know," said Benny. "But Laura needs our help."

"Well," said Violet, "it sounds really important."

Up front, Henry looked at the road map. The fourteen-year-old was telling Grandfather which roads to take to the farm.

The children liked taking road trips to new places. Laura and David Shea used to live near the Aldens in Greenfield. They owned the children's favorite restaurant, Applewood Café. Laura let the children help care for the restaurant's vegetable garden. Then the Sheas bought a farm and moved from Connecticut to New York.

"I miss Applewood's hamburgers with honey-barbeque sauce," said Henry.

Violet retied the purple bow on one of her ponytails. "I miss their pancakes with honey and powdered sugar," she said.

"I miss everything," said Benny.

"Look," said Grandfather. A big highway sign ahead said: Welcome to New York—The Empire State.

Soon they were passing open country fields. "I wish Watch could've come," said Benny. "He could run around without a leash."

"That," said Jessie, "is *exactly* why Laura asked us to leave Watch at home with Mrs. McGregor." Mrs. McGregor was their housekeeper. She took care of Watch when the family was away. "Bees and dogs just don't mix," Jessie said. "Watch would get into all sorts of trouble. Remember the time he chased that skunk?"

"P U!" said Benny, holding his nose.

"Take the next exit," Henry told Grandfather. "Then turn right."

Grandfather turned off the highway onto a narrow country road. Benny bounced in his seat. "Are we there, are we there?"

"Almost," said Henry.

The children once lived near a small road like this. After their parents died, they were scared to go live at their grandfather's house. They'd never met him before. What if he was mean? They ran away and hid in the woods. One night they found shelter from a thunderstorm in an old railroad car hidden among the trees. That boxcar became their new home. Then one day their grandfather found them. Grandfather turned out to be a kind, loving man. He asked them to live with him, and they'd lived together happily ever since.

"We're here," said Henry. They drove under a sign that said: Applewood Farm. Grandfather pulled up to an old farmhouse and everyone scrambled out. Henry unloaded their bags from the trunk.

"You can't park there!" A tall gray-haired woman marched toward them. "This is private property.

Parking for the store is down the road."

"Oh," said Grandfather. "Laura asked us—"

An old red truck rumbled up. Benny's eyes grew wide. The driver was dressed in all white—almost like an astronaut! Their head was even covered by a hat and veil. The person in the white spacesuit climbed out, calling, "Hello! Welcome!" As the hat with the veil came off, long black hair tumbled out.

"Laura!" cried Jessie.

Laura spread her arms wide for a group hug. "I am so happy to see you all," she said.

The gray-haired woman crossed her arms, frowning. "You know these people?" she asked.

"The Aldens are dear friends," said Laura. "They've come to help harvest our honey." She turned to the children, saying, "Everyone, this is my new neighbor, Zelda. She moved here from the city and took my beekeeping class last month. She's volunteered to help with our honey harvest too."

Zelda walked away, muttering, "Beekeeping is much too difficult for children."

Laura grinned at the children. "Oh, how I've missed you."

The Honeybee Emergency

"You told Benny you have an emergency," said Henry. "How can we help?"

"Actually," said Laura, "I have two emergencies." She pulled off her gloves. "First, I'm starting a bee-keeping class in two weeks for local children. But I've never taught children before. I thought since I know you all so well, I could practice my teaching on you. My second emergency is that David was called away on business. He'll be gone all week. I really, *really* need your helping hands to harvest our honey."

Jessie twirled a lock of her straight brown hair around and around her finger. "Will we work with real live honeybees?" she asked.

"Of course," said Laura.

"Will we wear spacesuits like yours?" asked Benny.

Laura ruffled Benny's hair. "Absolutely!" she said. "Except these are beekeeping suits."

"Count us in!" said Henry.

Laura gave them high-fives. "Thank you, thank you, thank you," she said. "You'll start after lunch. Right now, I have to check a few things in the pasture. You can go inside and unpack. There's a room at the top of the stairs with bunk beds that

I fixed up for you. I'll send Walt over to give you a tour. He knows this farm better than anyone. We'll meet back here for lunch."

Grandfather smiled. "I can see you don't need me. Laura, it's wonderful to see you again. I know the children are in good hands." He hugged his grand-children good-bye. "I have work to do back home," he said. "I'll see you all at the end of the week."

After Grandfather left, the children quickly unpacked. Then they went back outside. They were eager to see more of the farm. A man wearing faded-blue overalls and scuffed work boots stood waiting for them. His bushy white eyebrows and wavy white hair reminded Benny of Santa Clause. "I'm Walt," he said in a booming voice. "Laura asked me to show you around. Let's go."

Walt took long strides. They hurried to catch up. "Do you work here?" asked Henry.

Walt grunted. "This was *my* farm for fifty years," he said. "'Til I got too old. Laura and David came along and bought the place. I tried sittin' around my house all day doin' a whole lot of nothin'. But I got bored."

"I hate being bored," said Benny.

The Honeybee Emergency

Walt looked at the little boy with the brown hair as if noticing him for the first time. Walt grunted, then said, "I asked the Sheas if they needed help. And here I am."

Walt showed them Applewood's vegetable garden, tall rows of corn, pumpkin patch, and fields of wildflowers. In the distance stands of colored boxes stood along a fence. "Those are some of our beehives," said Walt. "There's more in the next pasture." He looked at the children. "Can't say I approve of putting kids and bees together."

"Didn't your children help with *your* bees?" Henry asked.

"Never did have kids," said Walt. "Don't know much about 'em."

"Oh!" Violet clasped her hands. "What's that?" A little white building with purple trim and a purple door stood near the road. Purple flowers grew all around. Purple was Violet's favorite color in the whole world.

"Gift shop," said Walt.

"It's so pretty," said Violet. "Can we see inside? Please?"

A bell tinkled as they entered. The children walked slowly around the small shop. There were jars of honey, baskets with honey-made soaps, honey body creams and lip balms, and boxes of honey granola, trail mix, and cereal bars.

A heavyset teenage boy was stacking cookbooks on a shelf. His bee-shaped name tag said: NOAH. "Can I help you?" he asked.

"Is everything here made with honey?" asked Benny.

Noah looked around. "Not the cookbooks," he said. "Or the tee shirts. Are you taking Walt's farm tour?"

"We are," said Violet. "This shop is my favorite so far."

"Have..." Noah's voice grew shaky, "have you seen the bees?"

"We're seeing them after lunch," said Henry.

Benny grinned. "We get to wear spacesuits! Um, *bee* suits."

Noah gulped. "Be careful...you don't want to get stung."

"We'll be careful," Jessie said. She wondered

why Noah worked so close to bees when he was obviously afraid of them.

Walt lifted a bushy white eyebrow. "Good grief, Noah," he said. "Don't go making people afraid of bees. Honeybees are just about the most amazing insects on the whole planet. You've never even *visited* our hives." Walt turned to the Aldens. "Let's go," he said, "time for lunch."

They reached the farmhouse just as Laura drove in from the field. Her face looked tight with worry. "There's a tear in the fence near the hives," she said, climbing out of the truck.

"Are the hives okay?" asked Walt.

Laura nodded. "They look okay."

The old farmer scratched his chin. "Could be a branch fell on the fence during that storm last night." He climbed into the red truck. "I'll go mend it."

Laura turned to the children. Her troubled face eased into a smile. "Anyone hungry?" she asked.

"Me!" said Benny.

"I thought so." She laughed.

CHAPTER 2

Missing!

Everyone helped set lunch on the big kitchen table. They sat down to a meal of honey-barbeque ribs, honey-roasted carrots, and fresh-baked honey biscuits. Laura set down glasses of lemonade. She also put four glass jars of honey on the table. "Honey tastes good on biscuits," she said.

Violet noticed the honey varied from light gold to dark brown. "Why are their four different colors of honey?" she asked.

"The color depends on which flowers the bees visited," said Laura. "This dark-brown honey comes from bees living in hives near our field of buckwheat. This light honey comes from hives near our clover."

Missing!

"How do bees make honey?" asked Benny. His face and fingers were smeared with barbeque sauce. Jessie handed him another napkin.

"Have you ever seen bees buzzing around flowers?" asked Laura.

"Sure," said Benny, licking sauce off his fingers. "Our dog, Watch, barks at bees all the time."

"Well," said Laura, "a bee's tongue is hollow, like a straw. Bees stick their tongues deep into the flowers and slurp up sweet liquid called nectar."

"Like this?" Benny slurped lemonade through his straw.

"Exactly!" said Laura. "Except only girl bees collect nectar. Boy bees—drones—stay in the hive with the queen." Laura went to a big whiteboard on the kitchen wall. She wrote: *Hollow tongue. Nectar. Worker bee (girl). Drone bee (boy). One queen.* "I'll add things as you learn," she said.

Jessie took out the small notebook and pen she always carried. She copied the words on the whiteboard.

Benny finished a second rib. "I sort of want another rib," he said, "but my stomach's too full."

"You need two stomachs," said Laura, "just like bees." She spread honey on a warm biscuit. "Honeybees don't have hands to carry nectar back to their hive. So they carry it in a special second stomach—a honey crop." Laura got up and wrote *honey crop=second stomach* on the board.

Henry thought about that. A honeybee's stomach seemed very, very tiny. "How much honey can a bee carry?" he asked.

Laura measured 1½ teaspoons of water into a glass. The water barely covered the bottom. "This is about all the honey a bee makes in its whole life," she said, writing the information on the whiteboard.

Jessie quickly copied down the bee fact. It was her favorite one yet!

After lunch, the children cleared the table.

"Did anyone leave room for dessert?" asked Laura.

Benny patted his belly. "I have room in my honey crop."

Laura laughed and cut them slices of honey cake. Someone knocked on the kitchen door. "Come in," called Laura.

Missing!

Zelda strode in. The neighbor was wearing a beekeeper's suit. "Someone damaged the pasture fence," she said.

"I saw," said Laura. "Walt's fixing it."

Zelda frowned at the Aldens. "Children can be allergic to bees," she said.

"The children used to help in my garden," said Laura. "I've known for a long time that they're not allergic."

Zelda turned and walked to the door. "I can see you're busy," she said. "*I'll* go check the other hives." The screen door slammed behind her.

Laura sighed. "I know Zelda seems rude," she told the children. "But she's just nervous about raising her first bees. Zelda used to own a big New York company. She retired here without knowing one single thing about farming or raising bees. Zelda took my beekeeping class, but she still has a lot to learn. Until you came, I was like her private teacher. She wanted me to give another beekeeping class for adults right away, but I wanted to do my junior beekeeping class first. Now Zelda has to learn to share me with you."

"I had a friend like that," said Violet. "She was jealous if I played with anyone else."

"I hope Zelda gets used to us," said Jessie. "That she doesn't mind you teaching us about bees."

Benny licked cake off his fork. "I still don't get how bees make honey," he said.

"Ah," said Laura. "So first, the bee slurps up nectar into its honey crop. When its honey crop is full, the bee flies back to its hive. Then it passes the nectar to another bee."

"How?" asked Benny.

Laura wrinkled her nose. "This may sound yucky," she said. "The bee throws up into another bee's mouth."

"Ew!" Benny made a face. "I don't like throwing up."

Laura laughed. "Then," she said, "that second bee throws up nectar into another bee's mouth. Each time, the nectar changes a little until it becomes the honey we love."

Benny finished his last bite of cake. "I guess I don't care *how* bees make honey," he said, "as long as I get to eat it!" He patted his full tummy. "Now can we wear bee suits?" he asked.

White beekeeper suits hung from a rack in Laura's den. The children pulled up the new suits over their clothes. Then they put on wide-brimmed hats and pulled mosquito netting down over their faces. They could see out through the netting, but bees couldn't get in. Next, Laura passed out gloves.

Walt had finished mending the fence, and the red truck was parked outside. As they walked to it, Laura said, "There are a couple of bee rules. First, always wear your beekeeper's gear around the hives. Second, stay calm and move slowly around bees. You don't want to startle them."

"It's a good thing Watch stayed home," said Benny. "He'd be chasing bees all over the place."

As they climbed into the truck, Henry saw the key in the ignition. "Couldn't someone steal the truck?" he asked.

Laura turned the key, and the old truck rattled to life. "I share this truck with Walt and Noah," she said. "Someone is using it all the time. It's easier to just leave the key inside. Besides, who would steal this old clunker?"

The truck bumped alongside a chain-link fence toward stacks of boxes. "Those are beehives," said Laura. Each beehive was painted a different color: yellow, orange, blue, green, and purple.

"Walt always painted his hives white," said Laura. "I thought I'd try colors."

"Can bees see color?" asked Violet.

"Yup," said Laura. "And they remember which colored hive is theirs." She parked along the chain-link fence. The *hummm* of bees filled the air. "Ready to meet the bees?" asked Laura.

"Ready!" said four excited voices.

The second they climbed out of the truck, bees landed on them. The children froze. Benny's heart raced. He moved closer to Henry. Jessie gripped Violet's hand.

"The bees are just checking to see if you're flowers," said Laura. More bees landed on them then flew away. Little by little, the children relaxed. One bee stayed on Benny's sleeve. Benny named him Buzzy.

They followed Laura to the blue-colored hive. Up close, they saw that the hive was made of four boxes stacked on top of each other. "I thought bees lived in trees," said Benny. "We had a beehive in our backyard once."

"That's how bees live in nature," said Laura. "Luckily, a man named Langstroth invented this kind of beehive. Now beekeepers like me don't have to climb trees to collect honey." Laura squatted, pointing to the two bottom boxes. "These are the brood boxes," she said. "This is where the queen bee lives. There's only one queen bee in a hive. She's the biggest bee and lays over a thousand eggs a day."

Henry whistled. "That's a lot of eggs!"

"Her only job," Laura said, "is to make sure the hive always has enough bees." Laura stood. "These top two boxes are called *supers*. This is where bees make honey."

"*Why* do bees make honey?" asked Benny.

"Hmm." Laura tried to think of a good way to explain it. "Do you have a place at home where you store food?" she asked. "Like cans of soup or boxes of pasta?"

"We have a pantry in the kitchen," said Violet.

"Well," said Laura, "these supers are the bees' pantry. This is where they store their honey. In winter, when there are no flowers to give them nectar and pollen, they eat this honey to stay alive."

Bees flew in and out of an opening in the front of the hive. Suddenly Buzzy flew off Benny's sleeve and disappeared into the hole. "That's the hive's front door," Laura said. "Let's move so we don't block their way."

Around the back, Henry walked to the chain-link fence several feet away. Henry could see where Walt sewed the fence closed with a piece of wire. The tear Walt mended looked big enough for a person to climb through. A few broken links lay on the ground. One had a piece of white fabric caught in it. Henry worried that an animal might eat the small pieces of metal. He put the links in his pocket to throw away later. Then he joined the others around the hive.

Laura picked up a metal can with a spout. "This is a bee smoker. It is a beekeeper's best friend," she said. She pumped the handle. White smoke streamed from the spout like steam from a kettle.

Missing!

"Smoke calms bees," Laura said. "That makes it easier for the beekeeper to work. Henry, please carry that top box, that super, over to the bench."

Henry lifted the box off the hive. "It's really heavy," he said.

"That's because it's full of honey," said Laura.

Henry set the super on the bench. Laura lifted its lid a little and squeezed a puff of smoke inside. As the bees quieted, Laura took off the lid. "Oh!" she gasped.

"What's wrong?" asked Jessie. The children crowded around. They saw six bee-covered wood frames hanging next to each other.

"Four frames are missing!" said Laura. "There should be ten." She chewed her lip. "This isn't good. This isn't good at all." She looked up and saw the concern on the children's faces. She didn't mean to frighten them. "I'll explain in a moment. First, let me show you a honeycomb."

Laura lifted a frame out of the super. It looked like a regular wood picture frame. Except instead of a picture in the middle, there were tiny shapes all joined together. "This is a honeycomb," she said. "These little spaces full of honey are called cells. Any honey you've ever eaten came from a honeycomb just like this."

Violet studied the cells. They all had six sides exactly alike. "Why doesn't the honey spill out?" asked Violet.

"Great question," said Laura. "When a cell is full, the bees make a wax cap." Laura poked her pinky finger through the pale wax covering a cell. Golden honey glistened inside. She eased the frame back into the super.

"Here's the problem," said Laura. She pointed to the space where the four missing frames used to be. A bunch of bees were building odd-shaped honeycombs all over the space. "These are burr combs," said Laura. "Burr comb is any honeycomb bees make where we don't want it. These bees saw the empty space and started building. Just look at their messy honeycombs. I must put this super back in order."

"Why?" asked Jessie.

Laura sighed. "Burr comb is messy and hard to get out of a super. Honeycombs in frames are

easier to harvest." She put the lid on the super. "My work here will take a while," she said. "Why don't you walk over to the gift shop. I'm sure Noah could use help."

The children put their beekeeping gear away. Then they walked over to the gift shop. As they went inside, two young boys chased each other out the door. A line of customers waited for Noah to ring up their purchases. The teen looked frazzled. "How can we help?" asked Henry.

Noah nodded at a box in the corner. "Could you unpack those tee shirts?"

The Aldens set to work putting Applewood Farm shirts onto shelves. While they worked, Jessie asked her siblings, "Did anyone notice the broken fence?"

Henry nodded. "Walt said a branch could have fallen on it," he said. "But I found some broken fence links on the ground. It looked like they were cut with some sort of tool."

"I wonder," whispered Violet, "if the cut fence has anything to do with the four frames missing from Laura's super."

Missing!

Before anyone could think about what Violet said, Noah came over. The Aldens were almost finished with their job. "Thanks," Noah said. "That was a big help. How was your beekeeping class?"

"Interesting," said Henry. "You should work with them."

"Me?" said Noah. "No way."

"Are you scared?" asked Benny.

Noah stared at the floor. "I don't like bees," he said. "I just took this job to earn enough money for school." New customers walked in. "I'd better get back to work."

"We have free time," said Henry. "Is there another job we can do?"

Noah scratched his head. "That back storeroom sure needs organizing," he said.

CHAPTER 3

Secrets in the Storeroom

Boxes, boxes, boxes. Small boxes, big boxes, boxes piled every which way. Boxes covered the floor, shelves, and tables of the small storeroom.

Jessie crossed her arms, tapping her foot. "This room does need help," she said. Jessie liked everything tidy. Back home, she organized her dresser drawers, closet shelves, Benny's toys, Henry's tools, and Violet's art supplies. This storeroom was going to take a lot of hard work.

Jessie pulled her long hair into a ponytail to keep it out of the way. "First," she said, "we'll mark the outsides of all these boxes. That way, people can tell what's inside without opening them."

She put Henry in charge of opening the boxes.

Secrets in the Storeroom

Violet found a thick, black marker to write on the boxes. After Henry opened a box, Benny looked inside. Benny told Violet what was inside, and Violet wrote it on the side of the box. "Jars of honey," Benny said. Violet wrote JARS OF HONEY in bold black letters. Benny looked into the second box. "Candles," he said. CANDLES wrote Violet.

When Violet finished writing on a box, Jessie moved it. She grouped each item together. Finally, every box was neatly labeled and put in its proper place. Jessie swept the floor while Benny held the dustpan.

Henry climbed a tall ladder. "There's a bunch of stuff up here," he said, brushing aside old cobwebs. Bottles clanked as he moved things around. Dust puffed up as he wiped the shelves. "It looks like no one's been up here for years."

Violet straightened piles of papers on the big desk. "Look," she said, holding up a stack of yellow papers. "These are flyers for Laura's beekeeping class." She read:

JUNIOR BEEKEEPING CLASS

- Become junior beekeepers
- Harvest honey made by bees in real beehives
- 4 week class for ages 10-18
- Learn all about these amazing insects
- Why do we need them? How do they make honey?

Applewood Farm
Call Laura at: 555-864-1246
Email: applewoodfarmfunwithbees@applewood.net

Benny frowned. "Ages ten to eighteen?" he said. "B—but I'm only six."

"Laura knows you," said Henry as he climbed down from the ladder. "She knows what a great worker you are."

Jessie put away the broom and dustpan. "Maybe Laura could take us into town tonight," she said. "We can pass out flyers. How many are there?"

Violet started counting. "Oh no!" she said.

"What's wrong?" asked Jessie.

"Only the top flyer is good. Someone marked up the rest with red ink." She handed each of her siblings a ruined flyer.

~~JUNIOR~~ BEEKEEPING CLASS

- Become ~~junior~~ beekeepers
- Harvest honey made by bees in real beehives
- 4 week class for ~~ages 10-18~~ *adults only*
- Learn all about these amazing insects
- Why do we need them? How do they make honey?

Applewood Farm
Call Laura at: 555-864-1246
Email: applewoodfarmfunwithbees@applewood.net

Violet blinked back tears. "It's not right to ruin someone's work," she said. "It's just not!"

"Who would do this?" asked Jessie.

Violet gathered up the stack of flyers. "We'll have to show these to Laura when she comes back."

Secrets in the Storeroom

They waved to Noah as they left the gift shop. Since it was such a nice day, they sat in big wooden chairs on the gift shop lawn. Honeybees buzzed around the shop's purple flowers.

"Why would someone ruin Laura's flyers?" Benny asked.

Violet slowly untied her ribbons. "Noah worked near the storeroom all day," she said. "He's afraid of bees. Maybe he wants to stop children from taking beekeeping classes. To protect them." She took her two pieces of purple hair-ribbon and wrapped them like bracelets around her wrist.

Jessie folded her legs under herself. She tried to think logically. "It is strange that Noah works here when he's afraid of bees, but I don't think Noah did it," she said. "He needs money for school. If customers don't come to visit the farm, the gift shop will close. Noah would lose his job. So he wouldn't do anything to stop people from coming to the farm. Besides," she said, "Noah seems nice."

Noah came out of the shop carrying a plate filled with light-brown squares. "The storeroom looks amazing," he said. "Thanks." He passed around the plate. "This is honey peanut butter fudge. I helped Laura make it."

They thanked him. "I've got to get back to work," Noah said. "The fudge is all for you."

The children let the sweet fudge melt in their mouths.

"I'm going to design a new flyer for Laura," said Violet. "I saw a jar full of colored markers in the office."

Henry was quiet for a long time. Finally, he said, "Someone's trying to hurt Laura's beekeeping business. Too many bad things have happened."

Jessie took out her notebook and pen and flipped to a clean page. "Ready," she said.

"Well," said Henry, "the first thing was the fence being cut."

"Then," said Violet, "four frames of honeycomb were missing from Laura's super."

"The flyers," said Benny, licking fudge from his fingers. "Someone drew on them."

"Who would want to hurt Laura's business?" asked Violet.

"Zelda's not very friendly," Jessie said. "And Laura said she seems jealous of us."

"But would she really hurt Laura? After all, Laura's been teaching her," Henry said as he reached for another piece of fudge.

"Walt doesn't seem to like us either," said Benny.

Violet patted her little brother's arm. "It's not us," she said. "Walt's just not used to having kids around."

When they finished the fudge, Benny set the plate on the arm of his chair. A few crumbs were left. A bee buzzed over and landed on the plate. The children watched the bee check a tiny crumb with its front legs. It played with the crumb awhile. Slowly, Benny slid the tip of his finger onto the plate. The bee looked over. It walked to Benny's finger and climbed on. Benny held his breath. He didn't dare move. He didn't want to frighten the bee. The bee seemed to be tasting Benny's finger. After a while, it flew away.

Benny jumped up, running around the chairs. "Did you see that? A real live bee climbed on my finger!"

"It was great how you kept so still," said Henry.

"What did it feel like?" Jessie asked.

Benny giggled. "It kind of tickled," he said.

Laura's red truck pulled up to the side of the gift shop. "We're over here," called Jessie, waving. Laura came to join them.

"Did you get the burr combs out of the super?" asked Henry.

Laura blew out a long stream of air. "It wasn't easy," she said. "Those bees wanted the burr combs to stay where they were." She sat on the grass.

"What did you do?" asked Violet.

"I pried out those messy burr honeycombs and pressed them into four new frames. Sort of the way you press clay into a mold." Laura said.

"Were the bees angry?" asked Jessie.

"They were a little upset with me," said Laura. "But I calmed them with the smoker and worked as fast as I could. When I finished, the four new frames fit right next to the other six." Laura stood up. "What have you been up to?"

They told her about organizing the storeroom. "I can't believe how many things are made out of honey," said Jessie.

As they walked to the farmhouse, Violet handed Laura one of the ruined flyers. Laura's eyes filled with tears at the flyer marked up with red ink. "Who would do this?" she asked. "Who doesn't want children learning about bees?"

Combing Honey, Brushing Bees

A new stack of yellow flyers for Laura's junior beekeeping class sat on the breakfast table the next morning. Violet had decorated the flyer with beautiful drawings of honeybees the night before. Then Laura printed lots of copies.

As the children finished their pancakes, Laura came inside the house. "I took some flyers into town this morning," she said. "I put them in the coffee shop, gas station, and grocery store, and I handed them out to people." As she set her bag on the counter, the phone rang. "Hello?" she said. Suddenly Laura was writing as fast as she could. She hung up, grinning. "I just got my first students!" she said. "A dad saw the flyer. He signed up his daughter and son. He's going to tell other parents about the class. Thank you, Violet." She gave Violet a hug. "Your drawings made my flyer stand out."

After breakfast they put on their beekeeper's gear. Laura, Walt, and the children climbed into Laura's truck. "Zelda's late," said Laura. "Should we wait?"

Walt ran a hand over his white hair. "People who are late," grumbled the old farmer, "don't respect other people's time. Let's go."

Laura turned the key. The old truck rattled to life. "Still," she said, "it's not like Zelda to be late."

Laura parked near the hives along the fence. Everyone got out of the truck. The children gathered around Laura. Bees buzzed everywhere, and Benny hoped Buzzy would land on his sleeve again. Walt lifted a white box out of the truck and handed it to Laura.

"This is an empty super," said Laura. She took off the lid so they could see there were no frames with honeycombs inside. "Today, we are movers. We're moving a couple of frames out of each hive and into this super. We're careful to leave enough honey for the bees to live on over the winter. Any questions?"

"If we take frames out of the hives," asked Jessie, "won't that leave empty spaces? Won't the bees start making burr combs?"

"Great question," said Laura. "As soon as you take a frame full of honeycomb out of the hive, you'll put an empty frame in. Full frame out, empty frame in."

"Full frame out," the children repeated, "empty frame in."

"Perfect!" said Laura. "Jessie and Violet, please carry this empty super over to the hives."

Walt went to the truck and started unloading ten empty frames. Henry picked up some and handed a couple to Benny. Walt grunted, as if surprised the children wanted to help. "Let me show you a secret," said Walt. He pointed to a tiny, red dot in the corner of a frame. "I mark our frames so we can always tell they belong to Applewood. No one notices the red dot but us." They carried the empty frames to the hives.

Combing Honey, Brushing Bees

"Let's start with the blue hive," said Laura. Henry walked to the hive and reached for the top box. "Whoa," said Walt. "I better lift it. That super's full of honey. It weighs around sixty pounds."

"I lifted it yesterday for—" Henry started to say.

"I'm tellin' you," said Walt, "that's way too heavy for you."

Henry didn't argue.

"Henry did lift it yesterday, Walt," Laura said as she walked over.

Walt stepped away. "It's all yours," he said, folding his arms across his chest. Henry gripped the super. Walt stared as Henry lifted the heavy box off the hive and set it on the bench. The old farmer didn't say a word. But Henry saw a look of respect in his eyes.

Laura took off the lid. Today ten frames were inside. "See those four nice, neat frames at the end?" asked Laura. "That's where I put the burr honeycombs. Tidiness makes a beekeeper's work much easier."

"Like we cleaned the storeroom to make Noah's work easier," said Benny.

"Exactly," said Laura. "Who's ready to brush some bees?"

"Brush bees?" asked Benny.

Laura picked up a long, flat brush. It looked like the kind they used to brush snow off grandfather's car. "We'll use this to brush bees off the honeycombs," said Laura.

"Won't that hurt the bees?" Violet asked.

"No," said Laura. "These bristles are as soft as paintbrushes. Watch." Laura lifted a frame out of the super. Bees covered both sides. With quick gentle strokes, Laura brushed away the bees. She quickly set the bee-free frame into the white super and closed the lid.

Laura picked up one of the new frames. "Benny," she said, "please put this empty frame into the space where the old frame used to be."

Benny slid the frame down into the super. "Full frame out," he said, "empty frame in." Bees covered his gloves and walked on his bee suit. Benny looked for Buzzy, but all the bees looked like Buzzy.

The children took turns brushing. They set the bee-free frames into the white box. They took just two or three frames from each hive. The rest of the honeycombs would give the bees enough honey to live on through the winter. It was Violet's turn to brush the bees when Zelda's shrill voice shattered the morning air. "You're brushing too hard!" The tall woman hurried toward the startled children. "You're hurting the bees."

Walt stepped in front of Zelda. "Leave the children be," he said. His voice was quiet but firm. "So far they're doing all right."

As the children worked, Zelda paced around them. "Humph," she would say. Or she'd mutter, "That's not how *I* would do it." She stood next to Laura. "Have you taught the children about swarms?" she asked.

"No, I haven't had time to—" Laura stopped. "Slow down, Benny," she said, going to the young boy. "Slide that new frame in *very* slowly. Give the bees a chance to get out of your way." She watched as he did it. "Good job."

Zelda followed Laura. "As I was saying," said Zelda. "You should teach about why bees swarm and—"

"Just a sec," said Laura, hurrying to help Henry put another full frame into the white super.

Zelda followed. "I'm afraid," she told Laura, "a swarm of bees could attack my new hives. All my bees might leave and—"

Laura turned to Zelda. "I really can't talk right now," she said. "My junior beekeeping class begins soon. I must learn the best way to teach children."

Finally, ten bee-free honeycombs filled the white super. Henry helped Walt lift the box onto the back of the truck. Walt covered the super with a green tarp. The tarp looked like the one the children used to make tents in their backyard. "Don't want bees finding these honeycombs," Walt said, pulling the tarp tight around the super. "They'll throw themselves a super-duper honey-eating party."

Laura drove the red truck past the gift shop and parked in front of a long, metal building. "This is our workshop," she said. "We'll harvest the honey here this afternoon. We can leave the super in the truck until after lunch."

The hungry junior beekeepers raced back to

the farmhouse to eat. A big box sat on the kitchen counter. EMPTY HONEY JARS was written on the side in Violet's handwriting.

"I asked Noah to bring in jars from the gift shop storeroom," said Laura. "This afternoon we'll fill them with our honey." The top of the old box was missing. Laura reached in and lifted out a glass jar. "Wha—!"

The jar was coated with black goo. She scraped the goo with her thumbnail and smelled it. "Blackstrap molasses," Laura said. She took out the rest of the jars. Sticky molasses coated every single one. Laura's shoulders slumped. "Walt left some old jars of molasses in the storeroom," she said. "One of them must have leaked into this box. What a mess. I'll go see if anything else is ruined."

The minute Laura left, Jessie filled the large kitchen sink with hot soapy water. Violet set the jars into the sink. It took the girls a lot of hard scrubbing and hot water to clean off the molasses. "Do you think Noah did this?" asked Violet. "There was no cover on the box. He must have noticed the molasses."

Jessie wiped her forehead with her sleeve. "He probably just grabbed the box labeled EMPTY HONEY JARS and never looked inside."

Henry and Benny picked up towels and began drying. "What about Zelda?" asked Benny, wiping a lid. "She was late this morning. She could have messed these up so it looked like we didn't do a good job cleaning the storeroom."

"Or maybe," said Henry, "this was just an accident. I was dusting around a lot of old stuff cluttering those high shelves. It was dark up there. I could have accidently knocked over some molasses while I was moving things around."

Walt banged into the kitchen. He seemed upset. "Where's Laura?" he asked.

"She's at the gift shop," said Violet. "Is something wrong?"

"A leg broke off that old extractor," he said.

"The what?" asked Benny.

Walt seemed surprised they didn't know what it was. "The extractor," he said. "It's the machine that spins the honey out of a honeycomb."

The children looked at each other. They didn't

say anything. But each of them wondered if someone broke the leg off the extractor on purpose. Was
this just one more thing someone did to stop Laura
from harvesting her honey?

Laura walked in and stared at the glass jars
sparkling like new. "I can't believe you cleaned
them," she said. "Thanks so much." She noticed
Walt's long face. "What's wrong?" she asked.

"Extractor's broken," Walt said. "Need to go to
town to buy a new leg. We won't have time to spin
out the honey today."

"Darn," said Laura. She looked at her hard-
working crew. "How about we all go to town and
buy a leg for the extractor. Then I'll treat you all to
ice cream."

"Yes!" said Benny.

"And," said Violet, "we can pass out more flyers."

CHAPTER

Stolen!

Early the next morning the children followed Laura to the farm's workshop. Yesterday Laura had parked her red truck outside the metal building. Walt had tightened the tarp around the super to keep bees out of the honeycombs. Now the children would learn to harvest the honey.

A rooster crowed as they walked past the gift shop. Dewdrops glistened on spiders' webs. Songbirds warbled in trees. Far away, a train whistled. The air smelled of wildflowers and ripe peaches. Benny raced ahead to be first at the workshop door. He ran around to the front of the building. "The truck's gone," he called.

"Very funny," said Jessie.

"I'm not joking!" yelled Benny.

They ran to the front. The red truck and the honeycombs were gone. Henry thought about the key in the ignition. Could someone have stolen the truck? "Do a lot of people know you leave the key in the truck?" he asked Laura.

Laura paced back and forth. "It's not really a secret or anything," she said.

"Maybe Walt came to work early," said Jessie. "Maybe he already moved the super inside."

Laura quickly unlocked the workshop door. The space was as big as a classroom. Tools hung from pegboards. Farm supplies were organized on shelves. Beekeeping supplies filled one end of the room. The white super with the ten honeycomb-filled frames wasn't there.

Henry noticed a jumble of odd-looking bikes in the far corner. "What are those?" he asked.

"Oh," said Laura. "Walt finds old broken bikes and takes them apart. He'll pull a good wheel off one, a seat off another, and handlebars off another. He says it takes about six broken bikes to make one good one. Then he gives them away to kids who don't have one."

"I thought Walt didn't like kids," said Benny.

"It's not that," said Laura. "Walt's afraid children will ruin or break something."

Henry rolled a bike into the middle of the workshop. It had a purple front fender, a red back fender, and an orange seat. The handlebars were rusty, and the peddles were two different sizes. Henry rode it around. "It feels pretty good," he said. "Would Walt mind if we borrowed bikes to go look for the truck?"

"I don't think so," said Laura. "I'll ride with you."

"Let's check the farm first," said Henry. "Just in case Walt or Noah used the truck for something. If it's not here, we can bike into town."

They sped past the vegetable garden and between tall rows of cornstalks. They circled around the pumpkin patch and under trees ripe with peaches. They kept biking until they reached the far end of the farm. Another farmhouse sat on the other side of the fence. Horses grazed in the pasture.

"That's Zelda's farm," said Laura.

Benny raced ahead. He glimpsed something red. "I see it! I see the truck. It's way over there behind that big tree."

They biked toward the truck. Suddenly Laura stuck her left hand straight down with her palm facing back. "STOP! STOP!" she yelled.

They screeched to a halt. Up ahead Benny stopped too. "What's wrong?" he called.

Stolen!

"See that black cloud over the back of the truck?" asked Laura. A cloud the size of a soccer ball hovered over the truck. "That's a swarm of bees."

"Are they dangerous?" asked Henry.

"Actually," said Laura, "honeybee swarms are usually calm. But I don't want to get too close until we put on our gear."

"Why do bees swarm?" asked Jessie.

"Usually because their hives get too crowded," Laura said. "Half the bees may leave a hive. They'll rest on a nearby branch until scout bees find a good place to make their new home."

Violet leaned over her bike's handlebars, staring at the big tree. "There's a big, dark blob on that low branch," she said.

"Good eye," said Laura. "That's where most of the swarm is. Those bees are crowding around their queen to protect her."

A few more bees flew from the tree to the truck. "I can't figure out who would leave my truck out here," said Laura.

A corner of the tarp fluttered in the breeze. "The tarp's coming loose!" said Jessie, pointing to the back of the truck. "The bees could get into our honeycombs."

Laura wheeled her bike around. "We've got to get home and suit up," she said. "We have to stop those bees from stealing our honey!"

They raced back and made it to the workshop just as Walt and Noah arrived for work. Walt glared at them. "What's going on?" he asked.

They quickly told him about the truck being moved and the swarming bees. "We're sorry we didn't ask permission to borrow the bikes," said Henry. "But you weren't here, and it was an emergency."

"You did right," said Walt. "What I *don't* like is that someone moved our truck. Too many people around, lately. Hard to keep track of things."

Noah was listening as they talked about the swarm. His expression was twisted with fear. "If you bring the truck back over here, will the swarm follow?" he asked.

Benny walked up and took his big hand. "Don't worry," said Benny. "I know how to be safe around bees. I'll stay in the gift shop with you."

Stolen!

"Me too," said Violet. "Laura asked me to decorate the store's signs."

***

Laura, Henry, and Jessie put on their beekeeper gear and met Walt at his black pickup truck. Walt had his bee suit on too. Henry helped Walt lift four old, empty hive boxes into the back. Walt tossed a white bedsheet, a peach, the smoker, and a large straw basket into the truck bed. "We're going to round up that swarm just like cowboys round up horses," said Walt. "Give 'em a nice, new home."

By the time they reached the red truck, half the tarp had blown off. Bees buzzed around, trying to get to the honeycombs.

"Hellooo," called Zelda from her farm. She stood at the fence dressed in her beekeeping gear. "What's going on?"

"Walt's rounding up a swarm," said Laura.

"I want to see." Zelda squeezed through an opening in the fence. "I need to learn how to trap bees."

Henry and Walt carried the four old boxes far away from the tree and stacked them on top of each other. "This is the bees' nice, new home," Walt said. "They just don't know it yet."

Walt lifted the lid off the top super box. Ten old frames hung inside. Walt handed Henry the peach and said, "Squeeze a few drops of peach juice on the tops of the frames. Then rub some juice outside the box right here." Walt took a red pen from his pocket and drew a big circle around the hive entrance.

"I'll do it," said Zelda, trying to grab the peach from Henry.

"Leave the boy be," said Walt.

Zelda huffed. "I'm just trying to help."

Henry picked up a small stick and poked a hole in the peach. He squeezed drops of peach juice on the frames. A couple of curious bees flew over. Meanwhile, Walt spread the white sheet on the ground in front of the hive. He lifted the top of the sheet and tucked it under the hive entrance like a bib under a chin. "I'm making sort of a bee welcome mat," he said.

"Zelda," called Laura, "we need help." Laura and Jessie had climbed into the bed of the red truck. They struggled to pull the tarp over the super. Bees buzzed all around. With Zelda's help, they tied the tarp tight around the super. A few bees were trapped inside. But most flew back to the swarm on the branch.

"Roundup time," said Walt, carrying the smoker and big basket to the tree. He set the large basket on the ground under the swarm. Then he gave the swarm a couple of puffs of smoke. The children gasped as Walt grabbed the branch and gave it a few really hard shakes. The clump of bees dropped right down into the basket.

Moving quickly, Walt carried the basket to the hive. He turned it upside down. The clump of bees fell onto the white sheet. Gently, Walt nudged a few bees up the sheet toward the hive entrance. The bees tasted the sweet peach juice Henry had rubbed on the red circle. Henry held his breath. Would the bees go into the hive or fly away? A few more bees crawled up to the entrance and tasted the juice. Little by little, the swarm moved into the hive.

"What happens now?" asked Henry.

"If they're happy here," said Walt, "they'll stay."

Laura, Jessie, and Zelda came to watch. "I want that hive," said Zelda. "After all, that swarm was nearly on my property. And I only have a couple of hives."

"You're a new beekeeper, Zelda," said Laura. "You still have a lot to learn about keeping bees safe and healthy. You don't want too many hives so soon."

"But you have so many bees," said Zelda.

Laura sighed. She could give this swarm to Zelda. But so many bad things could happen to bees—like sickness or attacks by other bees. The list was long. "You're not ready to care for more bees," said Laura. "Not until you can raise the ones you already have for one whole year." She looked around. "Let's clean up and get back to the shop."

As soon as they pulled up to the workshop, they took the tarp off the super. Laura brushed away the few bees left from the swarm. Then Walt carried the super inside. Laura set the tarp on the workbench. Then she went over to the super and lifted out the frames. The honeycombs were still full of honey. "We did it!" she said. "We saved the harvest!"

CHAPTER 6

Four Eggs-pert Detectives

They couldn't harvest the honey until Walt welded a new leg onto the extractor. Henry offered to help, but Walt said, "It's too dangerous. I'll have it fixed in about an hour."

Henry didn't mention that Grandfather had taught him how to weld. Back home in Greenfield, Henry was always fixing broken metal things for friends and neighbors.

Laura said, "I'll use this hour to start making dough for tonight's bread. Zelda's coming over to learn how to make bread. Why don't the four of you just relax?"

"Don't you have a one-hour kind of job we can do?" asked Jessie.

Laura thought a moment. "Actually, I do." She grabbed four wire baskets. "I didn't have time to collect eggs this morning," she said. "You can fill these. But don't stack eggs more than four rows high. You don't want to break the shells."

The children walked along the path to the chicken coop. Applewood Farm's chickens were free-range. They wandered everywhere and any-where on the farm. Laura said this made for happy, healthy chickens. They laid their eggs in a row of wood cubbies David and Laura had built. The cubbies looked like the ones at Benny's school. But instead of clothes and books, the Applewood cubbies were filled with chickens and eggs.

Chickens sat in a few of the cubbies. The rest were empty. Benny quickly went to the empty ones. He found two eggs in the first cubby. He carefully picked them out of the straw nest and set them gently into his basket. The older children began lifting hens off the nests to get to the eggs. As they worked, they talked about the strange things going on at the farm.

"Wait, wait, wait," said Jessie. She put down her

basket and took out her small notebook and pen. Jessie read them the list she'd written.

The fence near the beehives was cut.

Four frames were missing from the super.

Someone ruined the junior beekeeping class flyers.

Molasses was spilled on the glass honey jars.

A leg on the extractor was broken.

Laura's truck was moved near a swarm of bees.

"Well," said Violet, "I know Noah didn't cut the fence. He's too afraid of bees to go that close to the hives."

"I agree," said Henry, putting another egg in his basket. "And Walt probably built that fence when this was his farm. He wouldn't mess up his own work."

Jessie sighed. "All right," she said, "what about the four missing frames?" They tried to think who would have taken the frames full of honeycomb out of Laura's super. Noah wouldn't go near bees. Zelda had her own hives. Walt had no reason to take Laura's frames.

Henry snapped his fingers. "Remember I told you I found some fence links on the ground?" he said. "One link had a torn piece of white cloth. Whoever it was could have ripped their bee suit on the fence."

Jessie twirled a lock of her hair, thinking. "Maybe," she said, "it isn't someone from our list. Whoever cut the fence near the hives and stole the frames from the super could've driven Laura's truck to the fence near Zelda's farm. Maybe they cut *that* fence to get to Zelda's hives."

"I wonder if Zelda saw anything," said Henry. "She was near the fence when we found the truck." He finished the second layer of eggs and started the third. "I wonder why she was dressed in her beekeeping gear. It's almost like Zelda knew the swarm was there."

Violet fluffed the straw in a cubby. She picked out feathers to use in her artwork. "Maybe," she said, "Zelda had been working with her own bees. That's why she was wearing her gear." The ten-year-old always tried to find the best in people.

"You know what's strange?" said Jessie. "Yesterday Zelda kept asking Laura to teach her about swarms. Then today there's a swarm right near

Zelda's farm." Jessie checked her notes and sighed. "There's still the molasses on the jars, the ruined flyers, and the leg broken off the extractor." She tapped her pencil on the notepad. Solving a mystery was like putting pieces of a puzzle together. Jessie tried to think of pieces that seemed out of place. "Does anyone else wonder why Noah works where people raise bees?" she asked.

Benny jumped back as a hen flew off a nest right in front of him. He lifted out two warm eggs and put them in his basket. "Noah works here," said Benny, "to earn money for school. He told me this farm is close to his house so he can bike to work."

"Remember yesterday?" asked Henry. "Walt parked the truck at the workshop. Noah said this morning that he didn't like honeycombs left so close to the gift shop. He was afraid bees would come looking for the honey. That bees would come into the gift shop."

Jessie turned to a fresh page in her notebook. "So," she said, "maybe Noah took the truck and drove it as far away from the gift shop as he could."

Violet lifted straw off an egg before setting it in

her basket. "Noah's way too scared of bees to drive a truck full of honeycombs," she said. Some eggs in her basket were different colors and shapes. "These sure don't look like the eggs at our grocery store."

"Look at this egg," said Benny. He held up a golf ball.

"I found a golf ball too," said Violet.

"Maybe they hatch into baby golf balls," said Benny. He put the golf ball back in the cubby. He would ask Laura about it later.

"What about Walt?" Jessie said. "He doesn't trust us working with the bees. Maybe he's doing things to stop Laura from teaching beekeeping to other children."

Henry set a fourth row of eggs into his basket. "Walt doesn't like having a lot of people around," he said. "This farm was probably quiet when he owned it. He didn't have children running around. He didn't have a gift shop full of customers. He didn't give beekeeping classes."

Henry set down his full basket. He picked up Jessie's and went to a new row of cubbies. "Walt wants things the way they used to be," he said.

"But he never would have left Laura's truck where a swarm could steal the honey." Henry came to a large hen sitting on a nest. She looked at Henry and clucked. He slowly slid his hands under the hen and lifted her off. She pecked his arms a few times. "Sorry," he said, setting her on the ground. She walked away, clucking. Henry collected three eggs for Jessie's basket.

The children were quiet as they finished their work. Maybe Jessie's theory was right. And if someone stole from Applewood once, they could come back and steal again. If it continued, Laura might have to cancel her junior beekeeping class. She wouldn't want to put children at risk. Now more than ever, the Alden's wanted to solve the mystery. They had to work fast. Grandfather would return in a few days to take them back home.

In the kitchen, Laura and Zelda were setting their bread dough into bowls. Laura laughed when the children returned with all four baskets filled with eggs. "You are 'eggs-pert' egg gatherers!" she said. She saw how serious they looked. "What happened?" she asked. They told her their idea about someone stealing honey.

"I haven't heard about thefts near here," said Laura. "Zelda, have you heard anything like that?"

"Uh-uh," said Zelda, suddenly busy washing their bread-making tools.

Laura looked thoughtful. "You never know," she said. "I'll call the sheriff to see if other beekeepers are missing hives."

By the time the children washed up, Laura had talked to the sheriff. "So far," she said, "no hives have been reported missing. I told him about the four frames someone stole from me. I'll email my beekeeping friends and tell them to keep their eyes open."

Walt walked into the kitchen. "Extractor's fixed and ready to go," he said. "That is, if anyone here wants to harvest some honey."

"I do!" Benny jumped up and raced out the door. Everyone laughed and followed close behind. But, once again, the speedy six-year-old was first to arrive at the workshop.

The Spinning Spaceship

Benny burst into the workshop and skidded to a stop. A shiny metal barrel gleamed in the middle of the room. It sat on three legs like a spaceship ready to blast off. Except this spaceship had a crank handle on the side like Benny's old jack-in-the-box. He wondered if something would pop up if he turned the handle.

Henry walked in with Walt. "Is this the extractor?" asked Henry, running his hand over the barrel. Walt nodded. Henry knelt to see how Walt had attached the new leg. "This is a nice weld."

Walt hooked his thumbs in his overalls. "You know about welding?" he asked.

"Grandfather taught me," said Henry. "Of course,

I'm not as good as you, but I'm getting better." Walt raised one bushy eyebrow and grunted. Henry thought it sounded like a good grunt. One that meant Walt might be getting used to having kids around.

Laura and Zelda were the last to arrive. Zelda stayed near the door. "Okay," said Laura, "this is the day every beekeeper waits for! Today we're harvesting honey—taking the honey out of the honeycombs. It's called *extracting*. I'll write that on the whiteboard later. But first..." Laura reached into her pocket and pulled out a handful of little wax candy bottles. "Take some," she said.

"I love these!" said Violet, picking two purples.

"Who knows what keeps the syrup inside these bottles?" asked Laura.

"Wax!" cried Benny, taking a blue and a yellow.

"Right," said Laura. "And how do you get the syrup out?"

Henry took two greens. "I bite off the cap," he said. Henry bit off the wax cap and sucked out the sweet liquid.

"Beekeepers call that *uncapping*," said Laura.

"Today, we're uncapping the wax on the honey-combs to get out—to *extract*—the honey inside."

"Oh no," said Benny, looking worried. "Do we have to bite off *all* the honeycomb caps?"

"That's ridiculous," said Zelda, making a sour face. "That would be very slow and very messy."

Laura smiled at Benny. "We have a better way to uncap the wax." She waved Zelda over. "Come watch."

Zelda leaned against the wall near the door. "I'll stay here. I don't want to crowd your *students*."

Laura lifted a frame out of the white super. The honeycomb in the frame was covered with pale-white wax. She walked to a small table and picked up a long, flat knife with an electrical cord. "Beekeepers use all kinds of uncapping tools," she said. "Walt uses this hot knife."

Walt took the knife's cord and plugged it into an outlet.

"I don't understand," said Violet. "If we cut off the caps—um, if we *uncap* the honeycomb—won't the honey spill out?"

"Good question," said Laura. "The honey's too

thick to spill right away, but we still need to work fast." She walked to a large, plastic tub with a wood board across the middle. "Some honey sticks to the wax caps. It's pretty messy, so we work over this uncapping tank."

Walt carried the frame to the tank and stood it up on the board. He slowly slid the hot knife down the honeycomb, removing the wax caps. The sheet of wax curled off the comb like ice cream curling in a warm scoop. When Walt finished, the wax fell into the tank. Golden honey glistened inside the uncapped honeycomb. Walt turned the frame around and uncapped the other side. Then he put the frame into the extractor. The children looked inside the metal drum. It had six slots to hold six frames.

"This is our old extractor," said Laura. "We have to crank it by hand. Walt will use our electric extractor over in the corner. It's easier but not nearly as much fun. Now," she said, "it's your turn to uncap." She handed the children small rollers with handles. Rows of metal needles stuck out of the rollers like quills on a porcupine.

Henry held the handle and spun the roller. "This looks like the little paint rollers we used to paint our milk carton birdhouses," he said. "Except our rollers didn't have needles."

"It will be too dangerous for my junior beekeeping class to use the hot knife," said Laura. "But this great little tool works fast. I'll show you." She lifted another frame onto the board over the uncapping tank. She rolled the spiky roller up and down the honeycomb. The metal needles quickly poked holes in the wax caps.

Zelda crossed her arms, muttering, "This is going to take forever!"

But, in less than a minute, Laura uncapped every cell on both sides. She set the frame in the extractor. "Your turn," she said.

Henry set a new frame on the uncapping tank. Benny pushed his spiky roller up and down the honeycomb. He felt the spikes poke through the wax. Violet rolled the other side. When all the cells were uncapped, Jessie put the frame in the extractor. Then they all changed jobs, so they could have a turn doing everything.

The Spinning Spaceship

Laura noticed Zelda near the door. "Don't you want to try?" she asked.

"No," said Zelda, yawning. "I can see how it's done. I'll go check on our bread." She walked out of the workroom.

The children glanced at each other. Zelda was usually so eager about everything they tried to do. Why was she walking out on the most exciting part?

When they put the last frame into the extractor, Laura asked, "Who wants to turn the handle?"

"Me!" said Benny. He grabbed the handle on the side of the spaceship. Benny pushed the handle around and around. Little by little, the frames inside the metal drum began spinning around like horses on a merry-go-round. As they spun, honey flew out of the honeycombs, spattering all over the inside of the drum.

"It's like the Spinning Art booth at the fair," said Violet.

"Never heard of it," muttered Walt.

"It's so fun!" said Violet. "You squiggle paint on a spinning canvas. All the colors spin out, just like

this honey is spinning out from the combs."

Laura noticed Benny tiring. "Time to switch," she said.

As they worked, Walt uncapped all the other honeycombs and put them into the big electric extractor. With a push of a button, the electric extractor began spinning.

"That looks a lot easier," said Benny, rubbing his sore arm.

Laura set a big white bucket on the floor under the extractor. She covered the bucket's top with a strainer. "Henry," she said, "would you turn that spigot at the bottom of the extractor?" Henry turned the tiny faucet and honey flowed out. The strainer's tiny holes caught bits of honeycomb wax but let the honey flow through.

When the bucket was full of honey, Laura set it on the edge of a table. Glass honey jars were lined up and ready. "Here's what you'll do next," said Laura, holding a jar under the bucket's spigot. As she turned the spigot, honey flowed into the jar. She stopped when the jar was full. Then she screwed a lid on top of the jar and cleaned off any drips. Finally, Laura stuck an Applewood Farm honey label on the jar.

"That looks just like the honey in the gift shop," said Violet.

"And that's exactly where these jars of honey are going," said Laura. "Okay, now it's your turn." Laura stepped back as the children filled, capped, and labeled the jars. Soon they were all done.

"When can we eat some?" asked Benny. "I'm getting hungry!"

"You're always hungry," teased Jessie.

"We have one last very important job," said Laura. Benny groaned. "Don't worry," she said. "This time, the bees do all the work."

They put the ten frames back into the white super. Bits of honey still stuck to the wood frames and empty honeycombs. Henry lifted the super. It felt a lot lighter now that they'd extracted the honey. Laura led them far out into a field. Henry set the super down on an old picnic table.

"We don't want to do this last step near the house or workshop," said Laura. "You'll see why in a minute." She took the lid off the super. "Quick, take out all the frames and stand them on the table."

The children worked fast. "Let's go!" cried Laura, running. They ran after her until she finally stopped in the shade of a tree several yards away. "We can still see the frames from here," she said, sitting on the ground. "Now we wait and watch."

In a couple of minutes, a bee buzzed around the table. The bee landed on a frame. It seemed to be tasting the frame the way the bee had tasted crumbs of their fudge. "That's a scout bee," said Laura. "One of her jobs is finding food." The bee flew away. "She's going back to the hive to tell the other bees she found honey."

Benny said, "But bees can't talk."

"Not with words," said Laura. "They do waggle dances and shake dances to tell other bees what food they found and how far away it is."

Benny jumped up and waggled his backside while shaking his shoulders. "Like this?" he asked, waggling and shaking around and around them.

"Look!" Jessie pointed. "More bees." A few bees flew to the frames. They landed on bits of honey left on the honeycombs, frames, and super. More bees flew in. And more! In less than ten minutes, everything was covered with bees.

"Our work here is done," said Laura, brushing grass off her shorts. "By tomorrow those frames won't have one speck of honey on them."

"Well," said Benny, "if the bees can have a snack, can we?"

CHAPTER 8

Flashlight in the Dark

They followed the wonderful smell of fresh-baked bread to the kitchen. Loaves cooled on racks. "I cleaned up," said Zelda, taking off her apron. She put one fresh loaf in a paper bag. "I'll take mine home."

"Thanks so much for helping," said Laura. "Stop by the workshop and take a jar of honey."

"No, no, no," said Zelda, hurrying out the door. "I—I'm fine. Bye."

The hungry children washed their hands as Laura set out snacks. "Remember, we'll have dinner in a couple of hours," said Laura. "You don't want to fill up."

"I'm never full," said Benny. "Remember, I have

an extra honey stomach. A, um..." He searched the whiteboard for the right words. "I have a honey crop!" He took a couple of carrot sticks.

Jessie opened a container of goat cheese. She spread the tangy cheese inside a celery stick. "Mmm," she said.

There was a knock on the door, and Walt walked into the kitchen. "I cleaned up the workshop," he said.

"Thanks, Walt," said Laura. She put a loaf of bread in a bag and handed it to him. "This is for you. And take a couple of jars of honey from the workshop. You earned it."

"Thanks, I will," he said. "But first I'll go check the hives." He noticed the children listening. Walt cleared his throat. "Sometimes," he said, "bees get a little upset when we take frames out of their supers. They don't much like being disturbed. I mean, how would you like someone coming into your house and moving things around?"

"I wouldn't like that," said Benny, who had his toy cars lined up in his room exactly the way he wanted them.

Flashlight in the Dark

"Sometimes," said Walt, "it's three days before the bees calm down." He cleared his throat again like someone not used to talking so much at one time. "And," he said, "do you remember that big swarm we found this morning? I'm going out to check that new hive we put them in." He nodded toward Henry. "They went inside because they liked the taste of the peach juice Henry squeezed on the frames. Now I want to make sure those bees stay put. Don't want them swarming off someplace else. If we can keep those bees happy, they'll make us some fine honey. Just you wait and see. Well," he pushed open the door, "see you tomorrow, I guess."

When they finished their snacks, Laura worked at the whiteboard writing more beekeeping words and terms. Jessie got busy copying them down in her notebook. Violet and Benny sat at the kitchen table. "Do you want to go with me to the gift shop?" Benny asked Violet.

As they neared the gift shop, they saw the parking lot full of cars. Inside, there were people everywhere. Noah stood at the register ringing sales as fast as he could. Violet walked behind the counter. "I can bag while you ring," she said. She set a bunch of Applewood Farm bags on the counter.

"Here," said Noah. He handed Violet a stack of the yellow flyers she'd designed. "I've been putting a flyer in each bag. People really like these. I've heard them talk about sending their kids to Laura's class." Violet felt proud each time she put one of her flyers into a bag. With Noah at the cash register and Violet putting items into bags, the line moved much faster.

Benny walked around. All the shelves they worked so hard to straighten were a mess. Customers left jars of honey next to boxes of candles and T-shirts on top of books. Benny darted around, putting things back where they belonged.

When the last customer left, Noah leaned against the counter. "I'm pooped!" he said. "People always shop on their way home from work. Thanks for helping."

Violet looked at a display of jars of honey on the counter. "These are what we made today," she said.

"Was it hard work?" he asked.

"No," said Violet, "I mean there's a lot to do, but it was pretty easy with all of us working together."

Benny came over. "Why don't you like bees?" he asked Noah.

Violet's cheeks grew hot. "Benny!" she said. Sometimes her little brother asked people very personal questions. "Maybe Noah doesn't want to talk about it."

"It's okay," said Noah. "I got stung once. I was around twelve. I'd just mowed our lawn, and I was lifting a pile of grass clippings when—*zap*! A bee stung my finger. I've sort of been afraid of bees ever since."

"I was stung once too," said Violet. "I was barefoot, chasing our dog around the backyard. We ran through a patch of clover and—*zing*! I stepped on a bee."

"Mine hurt," said Noah.

"Mine too," said Violet. "I think part of it was the surprise. Not expecting a bee sting. I mean, I think it hurts worse when I fall off my bike and scrape my knee."

Noah laughed. "I fall off my skateboard *all* the

time," he said. "I'm always trying out new tricks. You can't learn skateboarding without falling."

"Which means," said Violet, "a little bee sting won't bother you. If you let Laura and Walt teach you about bees, you'll learn how to be safe around them." She thought of the bees out in the field, cleaning honey off the frames. "Benny and I were really close to thousands of bees today. And we didn't get one single teeny, tiny sting. Not one!"

Noah thought a while. He looked at the ten-year-old girl and six-year-old boy. If they could do it... "Maybe I'll try," he said. "I would like to learn more about how all this honey stuff is made."

***

After dinner Henry and Jessie walked outside. They hoped to see the Milky Way in the night sky.

A small light moved out in the field. "What's that?" asked Jessie.

Henry peered into the darkness. "Looks like a flashlight," he said. "Maybe Walt's still out checking the hives."

"Could it be whoever is causing trouble?" Jessie asked.

"I don't know," Henry said. "But we're running out of time to solve this mystery."

Suddenly a car door closed. "Sounds like someone's in the gift shop parking lot," whispered Jessie.

They walked over. The lot was empty except for Laura's red truck and a black car. They jumped as the car's engine roared to life. Its lights flared. As it sped away, moonlight shone on the driver. "Zelda!" said Henry. "What's she doing here? I thought she went home hours ago."

They looked around. The gift shop was closed. The only other building nearby was the workshop. "All the honey we harvested today is still in the workshop," said Jessie. "That's the only place she could have been." They checked, but the workshop was locked.

"It's too dark now," said Henry. "We'll look around first thing in the morning."

At bedtime, snuggled in their bunk beds, Jessie and Henry told Violet and Benny about the strange light in the field and about Zelda sneaking around in the dark. "She acted strange all day," said Jessie. "She didn't want to uncap honey from the honeycombs. She didn't want to crank the extractor. She left before we put the honey into jars."

Henry pressed on his pillow until it was the shape he liked. "Maybe the flashlight we saw was Walt checking the hives again," he said. "He's worried that we upset the bees when we took the frames out of the super."

Benny's sleepy voice said, "Full frame out, empty frame in."

Violet told them about Noah being afraid of bees because he was stung. And about how he wanted to learn more about beekeeping. "Maybe," she said, "we could help teach him."

"Full frame out," Benny's soft voice trailed into sleep, "empty frame..."

Connecting the Clues

Before breakfast the children went to collect eggs. Most of the hens were already up and out of the coop. Benny made sure a white golf ball was in each cubby. Laura had told him the hens thought the golf balls were eggs. Having them in the cubbies made the hens feel safe to lay their eggs there.

After breakfast Laura went to her office to make a call. The children walked to the meadow to see if the bees finished cleaning honey from the frames. Benny trailed behind. "Are the bees all gone?" he asked. He didn't want to get too close to thousands of hungry bees without his bee suit on.

Jessie took his hand. "If bees are still there," she said, "we'll come back this afternoon."

Connecting the Clues

But as they neared the table, they did not see one single bee. The children walked closer. Bees had cleaned every bit of honey off the honeycombs, super, and frames. "I wish I could train bees to clean my room," said Benny.

They put the ten frames back into the super. Four frames were left over. "Could these be the four missing frames?" asked Jessie. "The ones someone stole from Laura's super?"

Henry picked them up. Every frame had a red dot. "These are Applewood frames," he said.

"Why would someone steal them," asked Violet, "then bring them back?"

"To steal the honey," said Henry. "These honeycombs were full of honey when they were stolen. Now they're empty."

Laura drove up and climbed down from the truck. "How'd the bees do?" she asked.

"The bees cleaned everything," Henry told her. "And someone left your four missing frames."

Laura checked the dots. "These are ours, all right," she said. "But who could have left them?"

As the children helped load everything into the

truck, Jessie said, "Henry and I saw a flashlight out in the field last night. A little later we saw Zelda leaving the parking lot. Do you think she knows something?"

"There's only one way to find out," said Laura. "Hop in."

Minutes later they pulled into Zelda's farm next door. A black car sat in the driveway. They walked into the field and past the horses. In the distance they saw Zelda in her beekeeping gear, tending her hives. They stopped, waiting until Zelda saw them. She looked down at the ground and began walking toward them very, very slowly. Her beekeeping veil covered her face. When Zelda reached them, she lifted her veil. Henry saw a rip in her sleeve. A piece of white fabric was missing.

"You're the one who cut the chain-link fence!" he said.

Zelda crossed her arms, covering up the hole in her sleeve. She pursed her lips and then nodded. "I guess you figured it out. I'm sorry," she said.

"Why did you do that?" asked Laura. "And why did you take my frames? You have your own hives."

"But my hives are new," Zelda said. "You taught our beekeeping class not to harvest honey from a colony in its first year. You said the bees might not make enough extra honey to live through the winter."

"That's true," said Laura. "But why take my frames?"

"You were so...busy," Zelda sniffed. "Preparing for the new class and all. I didn't think you'd have time to teach me how to harvest the honey. I—I decided to try doing it myself." She wiped her eyes. "I cut the fence near your hives, so you'd think thieves stole your frames. I—I harvested the honey from your honeycombs. That's why I didn't take the honey you and the children harvested. I felt so bad, so I tried to return the frames, but there were always people around. I was afraid someone would catch me. Finally, last night, I sneaked into the pasture and left the frames with the others. I hoped you wouldn't notice."

Jessie tried her hardest not to feel sorry for Zelda. Zelda stole. Zelda lied. Zelda was pushy and rude. Still, Zelda looked so sad. Like she was truly sorry. Jessie couldn't help feeling a teeny bit sorry for her.

"That's not the worst of what I've done," said Zelda.

"There's more?" Laura's voice was stern. "I thought we were friends."

"We are, we are," said Zelda. "It's just...you got me so interested in beekeeping. I wanted to try everything right away. But you weren't giving another adult class. That's why I volunteered to help with Applewood's bees. I loved having you teach me every day. But then," she looked at the Aldens, "these children came. You didn't have time for me anymore." She blew her nose. "And when I asked you to teach me how to trap a swarm..."

Violet gasped. "That's why you parked the truck full of honeycombs near that tree full of bees?"

"Yes," Zelda said, "I did. I had seen the swarm the day before. I thought I could trap some of the bees by parking your truck nearby. I tried to catch the bees in a net as they flew to the honey. But I couldn't. And the swarm started to get under the tarp. I never saw so many bees! I didn't mean to let them steal your honey. I hid when all of you rode up on your bikes."

Jessie stepped forward. "Did you ruin Laura's flyers?" she asked. "Were you trying to stop Laura from teaching children?"

Zelda looked confused. "Flyers? I never touched any flyers." She took Laura's hand. "Please forgive me," she said. "I'll do anything to make this up to you."

Laura thought for a moment. "I'm pretty angry right now," she said. "And disappointed. I wish you had talked to me about this. But I do believe you're sorry for the trouble you caused."

"I am, I truly am," said Zelda.

"Okay," said Laura. "Here's what we're going to do. A lot of children are signing up for my junior beekeeping class. I'll have to give more than one class. But I can only do that if I have a helper. A good helper. Someone who knows about beekeeping. Sometimes," said Laura, "the best way to learn is to teach. Are you interested?"

Zelda smiled through her tears. "Really?" she asked.

Connecting the Clues

"Really," said Laura. "You'll start a week from Saturday."

***

Laura pulled up her truck to Applewood's workshop. As the children helped unload the frames and super, Laura looked at her watch. "Would you put these things inside with the bee supplies?" Laura asked.

As she drove off, Benny raced to open the workshop door. A piece of paper was taped to the door. He tried to read the words written in red ink. Benny was pretty good at reading books. But it was too hard to read handwriting.

Jessie went over and pointed to the words as she read them so Benny could follow along. "'Gone to mend fence between our place and Zelda's,'" read Jessie. "'Out where the swarm was. Walt.'"

Violet thought the curly way Walt wrote *a* and *s* looked familiar. "Wait a second," she said, running to the farmhouse. She came back waving a yellow sheet of paper. It was one of the ruined flyers. "Look," she said, pointing to the lettering. "This is the same handwriting that's on these flyers!"

Jessie snapped her fingers. "Walt used a red pen to draw a circle around the hive's entrance."

"I remember," said Henry. "I squeezed peach juice around that circle."

The children carried the frames and super inside to the bee supply corner. Henry strode over to the pile of bikes and pulled one out. "We need to talk to Walt," he said.

The four children biked across the farm to the far fence. They passed the new hive they made for the swarm. Busy bees flew in and out. They kept riding to where Walt's black truck was parked under the big tree where the swarm had been. He was mending the fence and turned when he heard the bikes. The children looked serious. "What's wrong?" he asked.

"We need to ask you something," said Jessie, holding up his note. "Did you write this?"

"Yup," he said. "That's my name right there at the bottom."

Violet held up the yellow flyer. "Did you ruin Laura's flyers?" she asked.

Suddenly the old man's face changed. He looked

like a small child caught doing something wrong. "I reckon you got me," he said. "I'm not going to lie. I did it."

"But why?" asked Violet.

Walt leaned against the fence. "I did it before I got to know all of you," he said. "I never much cared for kids. They're always up to mischief. You have to understand these bees are like my babies. I worry when they're sick. I make sure they're fed and have a good home. So when Laura got it in her head to teach beekeeping to children, well..." He raised his bushy white eyebrows. "I was afraid kids would hurt my bees. I changed Laura's flyer to look like the class was just for grown-ups."

"You said you marked up the flyers before you got to know us," said Henry. "Do you still feel the same way about us?"

Walt smiled, his eyes twinkling. "The four of you helped me see how much kids could do...and do well," he said. "Actually, I'm kind of looking forward to helping Laura with her new junior beekeeping class."

***

That night, there was a huge feast. Laura invited Zelda, Walt, and Noah to the children's farewell dinner. Laura said, "This meal is to thank you all for your amazing help! I could never have harvested all our honey without you."

"I'm afraid I gave you more trouble than help," said Zelda, "but I'm so happy to be here with all of you." She smiled.

Violet was surprised at how friendly Zelda now seemed. She hoped Zelda would be that way more often.

Later as Zelda, Walt, and Noah were leaving, everyone hugged. "I hope you come back real soon," Walt told them.

"I want to thank you," said Zelda, "for helping me make things right."

Laura watched in amazement. After the door closed, she said, "Do the Aldens always leave a place better than when they found it?"

Jessie smiled. "We try," she said.

Noah's Surprise

The next morning the children dressed and packed. As they finished breakfast, Grandfather's horn tooted. They ran outside, greeting him in their new Applewood Farm T-shirts. Benny's yellow shirt said, "bee kind." Violet's purple shirt said, "sweet as can bee." Jessie's red shirt said, "bee awesome!" Henry's green shirt said, "the bee whisperer."

Grandfather laughed. "I guess you liked working with Laura's bees," he said.

"We have a shirt for you too," said Violet. She handed Grandfather a T-shirt that said, "king bee."

"We learned there isn't really a king bee in a hive though," Benny told him.

"Thank you. This is just about the best shirt I

ever had!" Grandfather said.

Laura came out of the house. "Oh, James," she said, giving Grandfather a hug, "I can't thank you enough for letting the children come."

"Were they able to help with your honeybee emergency?" he asked.

"A thousand percent," said Laura. "I really couldn't have done it without them. Come on, we'll show you."

They led Grandfather on a tour, all talking at once. "Here's where we gathered eggs." "Those are the hives." "Here's the workshop where we harvested honey."

Inside the workshop the children explained about supers and frames and honeycombs and uncapping and extracting. Benny turned the crank on the extractor. "This is how you spin honey out of honeycombs," he said.

Grandfather watched, amazed. "I can't believe how much you've learned in such a short time," he said.

"Laura's a great teacher," said Jessie, who thought she might teach when she grew up. "Laura wrote everything on a whiteboard," she said. "I copied the lessons in my notebook. When we get home, I'll type them on the computer and print them out. I can pin them on our corkboard so we never forget."

"Would you like to see what your grandchildren made?" asked Laura.

"Absolutely!" said Grandfather.

They walked toward the gift shop. "When David was called away on business," said Laura, "I didn't know if I could harvest the honey without his help. Also I worried about the best way to teach beekeeping to children."

She opened the gift shop door. There were no customers this early in the morning. Noah wasn't behind the counter. Laura showed Grandfather a table filled with jars of honey. "Your grandchildren made all of these," she said.

Grandfather picked up a jar. "These look wonderful," he said.

Violet held up a jar. "These are my bee drawings on the new labels," she said.

"And I stuck the labels on," said Benny. "Some are a little crooked."

Laura smiled. "That's how people will know

they're homemade."

"Hey!" Noah came out of the storeroom. "I was hoping I'd see you before you left. Wait right there! Don't move! I've got a surprise." The teen disappeared back into the storeroom.

"That's my friend, Noah," Benny told Grandfather. "He used to be afraid of bees."

"While you're waiting," said Laura, "I'd like each of you to pick a gift from the shop to take home."

Jessie found a big candle made from the same beeswax as the honeycombs. She would share it with Mrs. McGregor. Every time they burned it she would think of her adventures at Applewood Farm. Henry picked a package filled with a large piece of honeycomb. Benny took a box of honey lollipops. He could eat one each night as his after-dinner treat. And Violet chose packages of honeybee stickers. She loved to put stickers all over her notebooks.

Noah came back into the store holding a piece of paper. "I filled out the form," he said, showing them. "I'm taking the junior beekeeping class. If my friend Benny can work with bees, so can I." Benny gave Noah a high-five.

The clock chimed. "We'd better start heading home," said Grandfather.

"James Alden," said Laura, "you haven't picked out your gift."

Grandfather looked around. He found a box filled with bee-shaped cookies and read the ingredients. "Honey, peanut butter, eggs, and whole wheat flour. Sounds perfect."

"But," said Jessie, "you don't like cookies."

"No," said Grandfather. "But Watch does." He pointed to the picture of a dog on the wrapper. "I think he'll like these doggie cookies just fine."

***

On the drive home Benny saw a row of beehives on a farm. "Bees on the left!" he called. From then on they all tried to be the first to spot stacks of hives. Jessie kept score in her notebook. Looking for hives made the ride pass quickly. Benny even saw a beehive behind a house on their block in Greenfield.

As Grandfather pulled into their driveway, Jessie read the scores: "Henry: nine, Violet: six, Jessie: five. And the winner," said Jessie, "with a grand total of ten, is the one, the only, Benny 'Buzzy' Alden!"

Mrs. McGregor opened their front door. Watch bolted past her to the car, barking. The children tumbled out. Watch jumped all over them, licking their faces, running around in circles, jumping on them again. Benny crouched down, letting Watch lick his face. Suddenly Watch stopped. He whipped his head around. He narrowed his eyes at flowers in front of the house. Bees were buzzing around, gathering nectar. Watch took off across the lawn, barking. The honeybees flew away.

Laughing, Benny ran over and threw his arms around Watch. "It's a very, very good thing you didn't come with us to the farm," said Benny. "Honeybees and kids are a good mix, but honeybees and dogs are not."

Turn the page to read a
sneak preview of

THE GREAT
GREENFIELD
BAKE-OFF

the new
Boxcar Children mystery!

"Henry!" Six-year-old Benny came running from the playground, across the green grass. He was shouting his older brother's name. "HENRY! HENRY! HENRY!" In his hand was a yellow piece of paper. He shouted for his sisters too. "JESSIE! VIOLET! JESSIE! VIOLET!"

"What's going on, Benny?" Henry raised his eyes from the book he was reading. The playground was close to where Henry, Violet, and Jessie had laid out their picnic blanket. This spot, under the old oak tree, was perfect for both watching Benny play and resting in the shade.

"The best thing ever is going to happen here in Greenfield!" Benny waved the flyer. He repeated with pure joy, "Best thing ever!"

"Well, are you going to tell us?" Twelve-year-old Jessie was cutting recipes out of a magazine and sorting them into a file box.

"Guess!" Benny challenged. He playfully tucked the flyer behind his back.

"Is it a new mystery?" Violet was ten. She stopped doodling with colored pencils on a drawing pad and studied Benny's face.

The Aldens were known around town for being great detectives.

Henry smiled. "It's been a little while since we solved a mystery."

"Sounds like fun," Jessie agreed.

"That's a good guess," Benny said. He pinched his lips and shook his head. "But it's not a mystery." He laughed. "Want to guess again?"

Henry was fourteen. The others looked to him as if he might know since he was the oldest. "Hmm," Henry rubbed his chin. "Let's see." He rattled off the clues. "Benny is excited. He's holding a yellow flyer. And it's not a mystery." Henry looked at his sisters. "What do those clues mean to you?"

"There's only one thing that Benny likes as much as mysteries," Jessie said with a wink.

The other Alden siblings said in unison, "Food."

Violet laughed so hard her two dark-brown ponytails shook.

"Yes," Henry agreed. "Benny loves eating." He stared at Benny for a long moment then added, "And contests!"

Jessie pushed back a strand of her long brown hair and thought about the possibilities. "It might be an eating contest."

"Remember the hot dog eating competition?" Henry said with a laugh. "Benny ate the most hot dogs and won first place."

"I think," Violet said thoughtfully, "since last year's town competition was a food-eating contest, this year's is probably—"

"A food-making contest?" said Henry.

Jessie turned to Benny and asked, "Is there going to be a baking contest in Greenfield?"

Benny brought the flyer around his back. He handed it to Henry with a smile. "One hundred and ten percent correct," he said. "The Aldens are the best guessers." Then he looked sideways at his family. "But are they the best bakers too?"

"Not me." Henry laughed while running a

hand over his thick dark hair. "I burned the toast this morning."

"I'm an artist," Violet said. "I'd rather draw a cake than bake one."

"Jessie can do it!" Benny said. "She made my birthday cake this year." He rubbed his belly. "And it was delicious! My tummy is still saying thank you."

Jessie was up to the challenge. "Tell us what the flyer says," she told Henry. "I could try."

Henry studied the announcement. "It's the Great Greenfield Bake-Off, a baking competition for kids." He checked the rules. "You need two people for a team. Everyone must bake desserts."

"I'll help," Benny said. "I can be the taster!"

"You can't eat everything I make," Jessie told him. "If we're a team, you have to be the sous-chef."

"The soup chef?" Benny licked his lips. "I do love soup."

"*Sous*," Jessie corrected. "It's a French word. It sounds like *sue*. You don't say the last *s*. The assistant to the main chef is called the sous-chef. For our team, you'd be the second baker in charge."

"I like it!" Benny cheered. "With Benny as sous,

Team Alden comes through!" He smiled and said, "It rhymes."

Henry, Jessie, and Violet all chuckled.

"Violet and I will be in the audience," Henry said.

"We can cheer you on," Violet said. "I'll make signs."

Excited about this new adventure, Henry, Jessie, Violet, and Benny went back to their boxcar to get started right away on the perfect recipes for the baking contest. Sign-ups were the next day, and there was a form to fill out.

The Alden children lived with their grandfather. After their parents had died, they'd run away and hidden in a railroad boxcar in the woods. The children had heard that Grandfather Alden was mean. Even though they'd never met him, they were afraid. But when Grandfather finally found the children, they discovered he wasn't mean at all. Now the children lived in his house in Greenfield. Their boxcar was a clubhouse in the backyard.

In the boxcar, their wirehaired terrier, Watch, was waiting.

"Watch!" Benny was excited to tell the dog about

the contest. "I'm going to be a sous-chef." Watch lay down on the floor as Benny explained what that meant. Then Benny whispered to Watch, "You can't help with baking because dogs can't bake. But I can sneak you some tasters if you want."

Watch barked happily.

"We need the right equipment." Jessie looked through a box of cooking supplies she had stored in a corner. "This isn't going to be like making snacks while we hang out." She pulled out some measuring cups and a big mixing bowl.

"The sign-up form is on the back of the flyer," Henry said as he grabbed a pencil. "You and Benny will have two rounds where you get to choose what to make and one round where the judges give you surprise ingredients, and you make what they say."

"Two original recipes," Jessie said. She told Benny, "Your first job as sous-chef is to help me think about what two recipes we are going to make."

"I like popcorn," Benny said as Jessie dug a cookbook out of the box. "And carrots with dip." He smiled and held up two fingers. "That should cover it. Easy-peasy!"

Jessie breathed a heavy sigh. "The recipes have to be desserts, remember? And those kinds of snacks don't use baking. Baking is special. It's about using heat, like in an oven, to make foods. We're going to need good recipes and the perfect ingredients. There's a lot of science involved to get everything to bake together just right." She opened her notebook and began to make a list of the dishes and tools she needed to get from Grandfather's kitchen. With every passing minute, Jessie was growing more and more nervous about the contest. She frowned and muttered, "This is very hard. So many things can go wrong. I could burn the dessert. Add too much salt. Or not enough salt. Or mess up the artistic decorations. Or..."

"You know what's also important in baking?" Benny asked Jessie.

She looked up at him.

"A no-worrying, smiling face," he said.

Jessie shook her head. "You're right!" She relaxed and smiled. "No more stressing. This contest will be fun."

"I know what the first poster for our team should say." Violet grabbed her markers.

"What?" Henry asked.

Violet chuckled. "Benny's 'sous-chef' cheer inspired me to write a rhyme."

"I can't wait to hear it," Benny said. "*Moo* rhymes with *sous*. You can use that. Or *chef* rhymes with..." He thought about it. "Nothing very cheery. Clef? Ref? Hmmm."

"I have another idea." Violet quickly wrote the words on a big poster board then held up their newest cheer.

Everyone chanted the words together: "Bake it with a grin. That's how the Aldens win!"

Continue the Adventures

The first sixteen books in The Boxcar Children® Mysteries
series are available in four individual boxed sets.

978-0-8075-0854-1 · US $24.99

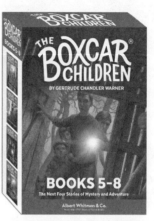

978-0-8075-0857-2 · US $24.99

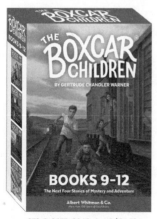

978-0-8075-0840-4 · US $24.99

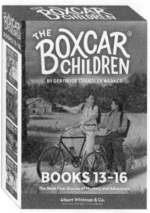

978-0-8075-0834-3 · US $24.99

THE BOXCAR CHILDREN®

An Exciting 5-Book Miniseries

**Henry, Jessie, Violet, and Benny Alden
are on a secret mission that takes
them around the world!**

When Violet finds a turtle statue that nobody's seen
before in an old trunk at home, the children are on the
case! The clue turns out to be an invitation to the
Reddimus Society, a secret guild dedicated to returning
lost treasures to where they belong.

Now the Aldens must take the statue and six mysterious
boxes across the country to deliver them safely—and keep
them out of the hands of the Reddimus Society's enemies.
It's just the beginning of
the Boxcar Children's
most amazing
adventure yet!

JOURNEY ON A RUNAWAY TRAIN

HC 978-0-8075-0695-0
PB 978-0-8075-0696-7

THE CLUE IN THE PAPYRUS SCROLL

HC 978-0-8075-0698-1
PB 978-0-8075-0699-8

THE DETOUR OF THE ELEPHANTS

HC 978-0-8075-0684-4
PB 978-0-8075-0685-1

THE SHACKLETON SABOTAGE

HC 978-0-8075-0687-5
PB 978-0-8075-0688-2

THE KHIPU AND THE FINAL KEY

HC 978-0-8075-0681-3
PB 978-0-8075-0682-0

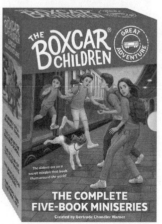

THE COMPLETE FIVE-BOOK MINISERIES

Also available as a boxed set!
978-0-8075-0693-6 • $34.95

The Boxcar Children®
Creatures of Legend

An Extraordinary 4-Book Miniseries

Join the Aldens and paleontologist Dr. Iris Perez as they investigate mythical creatures around the world!

HC 978-0-8075-0804-6 · US $12.99
PB 978-0-8075-0813-8 · US $6.99

HC 978-0-8075-0805-3 · US $12.99
PB 978-0-8075-0814-5 · US $6.99

HC 978-0-8075-0806-0 · US $12.99
PB 978-0-8075-0816-9 · US $6.99

HC 978-0-8075-0807-7 · US $12.99
PB 978-0-8075-0817-6 · US $6.99

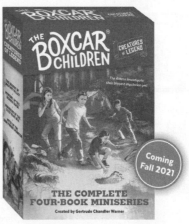

Also available as a boxed set!
978-0-8075-0827-5 · $24.99

Watch The Boxcar Children® Movies

Featuring the voices of Martin Sheen, J.K. Simmons, and Joey King

The Boxcar Children and *Surprise Island* animated movie adaptations are both available on DVD and select streaming services.

Download The Boxcar Children® Educational Augmented Reality App

Watch and listen to your favorite characters as they spring from the pages to act out scenes, ask questions, and encourage a love of reading. The app works with any paperback or hardcover copy of the first book in the series, printed after 1942.

The Boxcar Children,
Fully Illustrated!

This fully illustrated edition celebrates Gertrude Chandler Warner's timeless story. Featuring all-new full-color artwork as well as an afterword about the author, the history of the book, and The Boxcar Children® legacy, this volume will be treasured by first-time readers and longtime fans alike.

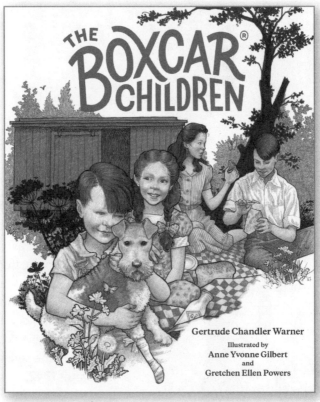

Gertrude Chandler Warner

Illustrated by
Anne Yvonne Gilbert
and
Gretchen Ellen Powers

978-0-8075-0925-8 · US $34.99

The Boxcar Children® Interactive Mysteries

An Immersive 4-Book Miniseries

Help the Aldens crack the case in these interactive, choose-your-path-style mysteries.

PB 978-0-8075-2850-1 · US $6.99

PB 978-0-8075-2860-0 · US $6.99

PB 978-0-8075-2862-4 · US $6.99

PB 978-0-8075-2857-0 · US $6.99

Also available as a boxed set!

978-0-8075-2854-9 · $24.99

GERTRUDE CHANDLER WARNER discovered when she was teaching that many readers who like an exciting story could find no books that were both easy and fun to read. She decided to try to meet this need, and her first book, *The Boxcar Children*, quickly proved she had succeeded.

Miss Warner drew on her own experiences to write the mystery. As a child she spent hours watching trains go by on the tracks opposite her family home. She often dreamed about what it would be like to set up housekeeping in a caboose or freight car—the situation the Alden children find themselves in.

While the mystery element is central to each of Miss Warner's books, she never thought of them as strictly juvenile mysteries. She liked to stress the Aldens' independence and resourcefulness and their solid New England devotion to using up and making do. The Aldens go about most of their adventures with as little adult supervision as possible—something else that delights young readers.

Miss Warner lived in Putnam, Connecticut, until her death in 1979. During her lifetime, she received hundreds of letters from girls and boys telling her how much they liked her books.